Favourite Things

Liz Ringrose

Website: lizringrose.co.uk

Artwork by Little End Creations

To Caro,

with love

Chapter One

He's standing apart from the group, his hands resting on the wall and although his eyes are cast down towards the beautiful city below us I can tell he's not looking at the view. His shoulders sag and his eyebrows are drawn together in an expression that is more sad than puzzled. Well, Kirsty, I tell myself. It's your job to ensure they're all happy. My passenger list tells me his name is Mike Hayes. Most of the tourists are in pairs or groups but he has come alone. I give him my cheeriest smile but he doesn't return it.

"Are you enjoying the Sound of Music tour, Mr Hayes?"

"I am. Thank you." His voice is flat and disinterested. Behind us a group of Japanese teenage girls photograph each other with the city's many church towers as a backdrop.

I try again. "Is this your first trip to Salzburg?"

"No."

A quick glance at my watch and I realise we need to return to the coach so trying to draw him out will have to wait. I steer the group back into the lifts which will take us back down through the mountain to street level.

We have a nice crowd this morning. There's the usual sprinkling of Japanese girls, American ladies, a few couples, a middle-aged nun and Mike Hayes who, I'm guessing now, must have regretted signing up for the tour. I check no one is left behind and take a last look at the view. Beyond the huge fortress, high on its rock, the mountains still have snow on top even though it's May and so warm I might have to loosen the laces on my bodice when nobody's looking. I love my dirndl costume with its pretty lace blouse and sprigged skirt. It's much better than the black leggings I used to slob around in at home.

Our coach is parked close to the painted horse pond. It takes me a few minutes to round up my party as they whip out their cameras and take photos of each other in front of the colourful frieze of rearing stallions.

"Get a load of Mr Grumpy," I whisper to Anton, our driver. I roll my eyes towards Mike Hayes who is sitting in the front seat next to the nun, looking more uncomfortable by the minute.

Anton gives me a tiny wink. He's a good laugh. We're both new to the company and we're the same age although he looks a bit older than twenty-five. Maybe it's the stress of looking after his sister that has aged him. He told me she's going through that difficult teenage phase and since their mum died there are just the two of them. I don't remember being a difficult teenager myself. I think my mother would say I'm having my rebellion in my twenties.

After doing a head count I turn on the microphone and when Anton steers us into the traffic I begin my spiel. I more or less know it off by heart but you can bet if I make a mistake someone on the coach will put me straight. Sound of Music fans really know their stuff especially the American ones. As we head out of the city I set the DVD going. Some of them sing along, some chatter and take photographs as the scenery becomes even more beautiful and the first of the Salzkammergut lakes comes into view. I notice the nun take out her cell phone and begin texting. I imagine another phone chirruping in a convent somewhere.

I could never see myself as a nun; and the thought of seven children is enough to send me sprinting to the family planning clinic so I'm not really sure what makes me love The Sound of Music so much. Maybe it reminds me of Christmas as a child, sitting on the sofa, clutching my latest Barbie while Mum and Gran, tissues at the ready, sang about their favourite things and swooned over Captain Von Trapp.

"I've seen the film twenty-odd times, Kirsty" Gran would say to me, "and it still makes me cry."

Now I'm living what surely would be Gran's dream, in Salzburg and working as a guide on this tour. I wish she was still around to wish me luck especially as Mum's reaction to my leaving England was not encouraging, and as for Jake, well, I'd rather not think about him right now.

Just before the village of St Gilgen Anton pulls into a lay-by on a high mountain road. Those seated on the right hand side of the coach gasp with pleasure as they have their first glimpse of Lake

Wolfgang stretching into the distance with mountains beyond. All the passengers except Mike Hayes get off to take photographs.

"We're so lucky today," I say, to him, "last week the weather was awful and we could hardly see the lake from here."

He stays in his seat but gives me a half smile. "It's a great view," he says, "but I've seen it before."

Anton and I dutifully stand beside members of the group while their friends take our photograph.

"There are photos of us all over the world," he says through gritted teeth.

"So let's make them good ones," I reply, widening my smile.

Moments later the nun sidles up to me. "I feel pretty stupid," she whispers in a Bronx accent. "People back home told me I had to dress up for this."

Even though the coach is air-conditioned she has beads of sweat on her forehead. She hoists up her habit a couple of inches to reveal trainers and socks.

"Often people do dress up," I say, in what I hope is a soothing voice, "although you seem to be the only one today. But I thought you were a nun so perhaps the others do too."

She doesn't seem appeased and runs a finger under the edge of her wimple. "But I'm boiling up inside this thing."

"Is there anything you could change into?" I'm trying not to laugh as Anton herds the teenage girls back onto the coach as though they are a flock of excitable sheep.

"Heck yes," say's the reluctant sister. "I have shorts and a shirt in my bag."

"Well, if you can stand it for a while longer I know somewhere you can change."

She looks relieved as she flops into her seat beside an impassive Mike Hayes and we take to the road again.

The cathedral at Mondsee is a wonderful sight and even though I've seen it dozens of times I understand why the tissues come out at this point of the tour. The towers of the salmon pink façade reach high into the sky. Anton makes his escape, driving the bus down to the lakeside while the rest of us file into the ancient basilica. I hang back as the others dab their eyes and walk in the footsteps of Julie Andrews, up the aisle towards the altar where she finally claimed her captain. Thoughts of Jake back in England dart into my head but I push them away. I take the nun to one side.

"There's a café across the square. Change in the toilets and put your nun's outfit in this." I hand her the large carrier bag in which I keep my spare dirndl. She gives me a grateful smile and hurries away.

I look around for Mike Hayes but he's nowhere to be seen. I don't think he followed us into the church but this is the point in the tour when the group members have free time so maybe he's gone exploring. Nobody seems to have any questions for me so I take a path leading up a hill behind the cathedral, towards the little folk museum. Finding a shady spot under the flower-laden bows of a horse chestnut tree I sit for a while and take in the view of the village and its moon-shaped lake; beyond it are the ever present mountains.

I feel unsettled today and Mike Hayes is the cause. I don't understand why he came on a trip that patently doesn't interest him. He's very good looking in a serious, intelligent sort of way. I have already noticed he doesn't wear a ring. His blonde hair is long and swept back. He's wearing chinos and a navy linen jacket so he's made an effort to look nice. I wonder if his girlfriend cancelled at the last minute and he was left to do the tour alone. That would certainly account for his disinterest.

I make a quick call to my boss and tell her there are no problems. I don't bother to mention the gorgeous grump or the overheated nun. Mariette is a great employer. She and her husband Karl own a few gift shops in the city and started up the tour business a couple of years back. There are two other Sound of Music tour companies in the city but the number of fans flocking to Salzburg each year means there's plenty of work for all of us. I think it must have been my enthusiasm for the film that made them give me the job. It is such a lovely story with the sort of romance we all long for, I suppose. Of course not all romantic stories work out so well; I thought Jake was my Captain Von Trapp but there was no happy ending for us.

Most of the party have had coffee and cake when I return to round them up and they are quieter as they board the coach for the homeward journey. If Mike Hayes is surprised that the nun by his side has morphed into a red haired lady in pink shorts and a blue shirt, he doesn't show it.

"In case you wondered where he was," Anton's head inclines slightly towards our silent passenger, "he spent the afternoon sitting by the lake."

I move a little closer to Anton as he drops his voice, he always wears delicious cologne and I keep meaning to ask him the name of it.

"I don't think Mr Hayes is a happy man at all," he says. "He just sat on a bench staring out at the water. He didn't move for an hour."

There isn't much singing as we head along the autobahn back to the city. The Japanese girls are letting their eyes close. Mike Hayes turns his head to the window and it's impossible to read his expression. 'Oh dear,' I tell myself, 'you can't win them all.'

As usual the passengers have taken up a little collection for Anton. He smiles his appreciation as he helps them all down from the coach then we pose for a few more photos.

"You don't fancy a coffee or something do you?" I ask him. I can't explain why but I don't feel like going back to my apartment just yet.

Anton's cheeks turn pink and he stares at the floor for a few seconds. "I'm sorry, Kirsty, I have a date; a girl I've liked for ages. I can't believes she said yes and … anyway, I must go home and make Vanessa something to eat first."

definitely something going on with him. He's beginning to creep me out."

Its obvious Anton doesn't quite understand my English slang but after lighting a candle in remembrance of his mother he whispers, "While you're in here I'll go out and talk to him."

When we all emerge into the sunshine again Anton raises his shoulders in a shrug.

"Mr Hayes says he will wait for us by the coach. I tried to talk to him but he doesn't want to speak to anyone. You are right, he is strange. Maybe we should ask Karl or Mariette what to do."

At the end of the following day, as we bid our passengers goodbye and Mike Hayes gives us that unenthusiastic smile we've grown used to, we take the bus back to its overnight parking space. Anton isn't his usual chirpy self; in fact we're both a bit thoughtful as we walk to the tour office.

Mariette pours us mugs of coffee and I explain about our strange tourist.

"Is he rude to you?" she asks.

"No. He doesn't say anything at all, that's the problem. He's on the bus every day but he doesn't join in with the fun or speak to the other passengers."

Anton puts down his coffee. "Today I asked him why he comes on the tour so much and he just said he enjoys it."

Mariette frowns at her computer screen. "Well, I have to tell you he's signed up again for tomorrow."

I don't bother to stifle my groan.

"I see it is a tricky problem for you," she says, "but he has paid his money and you say he isn't offensive. I don't see how we can tell him he cannot join the tour."

We all stare into our coffee for a few moments then she continues, "If he is impolite or makes you feel uncomfortable you must ring me immediately; but if not, try and make a joke of it."

I don't feel much like laughing as Anton and I walk to the city bus station. He doesn't seem very amused either.

"How are things going with your new girlfriend?" I ask. His smile is half-hearted. "She met Vanessa last night and it did not go so well. Barbara tried to be friendly but Vanessa ignored her all through dinner and as soon as she'd eaten she called her friends and went out."

"You don't think she'll put Barbara off do you?"

"Who knows?" He's looking really fed up now. "Vanessa is angry with me. I must take a taxi driving job a couple of evenings a week. My salary on the tour is not enough to pay all the bills. She thinks I don't care about her but it is for her that I do all this work."

"But you won't leave her on her own in the evenings?"

"Of course not," he looks affronted. "My good neighbour, Lotte, will sit with her. But Vanessa says she is too old to need a nanny."

Obliquely I think of the oldest Von Trapp girl in The Sound of Music, saying a similar thing, but it certainly isn't the right time to say something so flippant.

"You'll be worn out doing all that driving," I say instead.

He gives me his wide smile and he's good old Anton again.

It's still warm when I reach my apartment and I fling open the windows. It's more of a bedsit really but it has a great view of the mountains and it's just a few bus stops out of the city.

"Why on earth do you want to live like that?" my mother had said when I sent her a photo of it. "Really Kirsty, you're the bitter end. You could have been living in a lovely flat in London; in Docklands, no less."

I wonder if she'll ever forgive me for not marrying Jake. But what can you do when you realise he's not the one? How would the film have ended if the captain had married the baroness instead of Maria? Besides, I'm a country girl. Nature and scenery are my favourite things. Growing up in the Peak District I was used to open spaces and even if those hills are now alive with the sound of hikers and Jack Russells, I'd choose them over London every time. I don't know how Jake could expect me to just slot into his stockbroker lifestyle?

Chapter Three

Next morning who should be waiting at my bus stop but Anton's sister Vanessa, with a couple of her friends. Now, I quite like the ripped jeans look but hers are positively shredded. The knee that protrudes from one of the holes has an exotic flower drawn on it. I've met her a couple of times when she's come to meet Anton from work but now, as I catch her eye and smile, she shifts her gaze to some point behind my head and adjusts the volume on her iPod. She has two rings through one nostril and another through her bottom lip which she nibbles constantly. Her dyed hair is aubergine. One of her friends is chewing gum and when the bus arrives she whips it out and sticks to the side of the shelter. As they all get on I realise they're heading in the opposite direction to Vanessa's school.

I say nothing about it to Anton as I board the tour coach an hour later. He's already looking tired.

At our first pick up point Mike Hayes also looks exhausted. His linen jacket is crumpled and his blonde hair is not nearly as neat as he takes his usual front seat. I stifle the urge to suggest he do the commentary as by now he must know it by heart.

Today on the tour we have an English lady with an encyclopaedic knowledge of The Sound of Music who wants to impart information to the other passengers. Several times I have to speak over her as she interrupts me. We all stream into St Peter's cemetery, one of my favourite stops on the tour. The peaceful, well-tended graveyard is always full of flowers and, in the searing heat, is an oasis of coolness as it nestles against the rocks of the Monchsberg hill.

"The film makers loved this cemetery and it influenced the escape scene in the abbey," I say as I gesture to the baroque porticos behind whose wrought iron gates the great and the good of Salzburg are buried. "These tall memorial stones are just like the ones the Von Trapp family hides behind towards the end of the film."

"Except they built a set and filmed it all in Hollywood," the English lady adds.

"Quite so," I say, trying not to grind my teeth."

"And at the end, when they're supposed to be escaping, they're actually just over the border in Germany," she continues, "and you can see Salzburg airport in the background."

"Why don't you just let Kirsty tell us?" Mike Hayes is facing the woman, his expression angry. "It's so annoying with you butting in all the time."

Other tourists nod and mumble their agreement.

The woman's face turns beetroot red and looks as though she might burst into tears. I suggest the others take a look at the cemetery and meet us at the gates.

"Sorry I overstepped the mark," she tells me, pulling out a hankie and wiping her hot face. I'm just a Sound of Music addict and I'm so excited to be here.'

"Don't worry," I say, trying to soothe her, "It's wonderful that you know so much about the film. Perhaps you could write a review of the tour for us and put it on our website." She seems appeased by this suggestion and I stay beside her as she photographs almost every wrought iron grave marker in the cemetery.

I notice Mike Hayes has vanished and minutes later when we re-join the coach, Anton tells me he has returned to his hotel.

"He said he was feeling unwell. I offered to call a taxi for him but he just walked away."

"Oh dear, well I'm definitely going to talk to him tomorrow," I whisper back, "I need to find out what his problem is. It's getting beyond a joke if he starts upsetting the other passengers."

Late in the afternoon, as we're heading back from Mondsee, Mariette rings to say she's leaving the office early.

"Would you be an angel and count the cash for me, Kirsty? Also you could print out tomorrow's passenger list and lock up."

I can hear a smile in her voice. "And guess what? Mr Hayes hasn't put his name down for tomorrow."

"How frustrating," I say to Anton as we pull off the autobahn. "Just when I decide to talk to him it seems he's had enough of us. Now we'll never know what his story is."

In the office I think about Mike's impatient outburst and wonder if he really is ill. Anton had made that joke about him fancying me and he *had* leapt to my defence this morning, silencing the woman who kept interrupting. 'But that's just daft,' I tell myself as I log out of the computer and turn it off, 'he's never given the slightest hint that he likes me in that way.'

I put the petty cash box into the safe and then, in the tiny kitchen, I rinse our mugs under the tap. Through the window I can see grey clouds gathering over the mountains and I hope we won't have rain for tomorrow's tour. I feel quite important as I leave the office and lock up. It's flattering to know Mariette trusts me.

On the way to the bus I decide to send Anton a quick text wishing him luck. Tonight will be his first shift driving the taxi but I find my phone is missing. After checking pockets and rummaging in my bag I remember I've left it on Mariette's desk.

It feels strange letting myself into the office and although it's only been a few minutes already the cloudy sky has darkened, leaving reception full of shadows. As I put my hand on the office door handle I hear a noise and hold my breath. It sounds like the whirr of the computer but I'm sure I turned it off.

Confused I push open the door. A figure is silhouetted against the window. Tall. Male.

I can't move; my muscles don't respond. I draw breath in ready to scream but before the sound can emerge the man moves, darting around the desk and clamps a hand over my mouth.

Chapter Four

Terror makes my knees buckle and I slump back against the door. Still with his hand over my mouth he pulls me up and I'm staring at the anxious face of Mike Hayes. He hisses into my ear, "Please don't scream, Kirsty. I'm not a thief and I won't hurt you. I'll explain why I'm here but promise me you won't scream."

I'm not at all sure I won't scream, but I nod and he takes his hand away. My heart is drumming a salsa beat in my chest.

"I'm so sorry to scare you." Actually he really *does* look sorry.

"Why? ... What? ... What are you doing here?" My words tumble out between gasps. I lunge forward, grab my phone from the desk and hold it against my chest.

"I just need to look at the computer. You could help me; we could use your password to get me in."

"Wait a minute!" My fear is turning to anger now. "I want to know how and why you broke into our office." I jab an accusing finger at him and I'm amazed to see him sag a little as he moves to the window.

"I didn't break in. I came earlier and saw your boss go down the corridor. I hid in that store room." He gestures to the door in the corner.

"You mean you were lurking in there when I was counting ...?" A wave of new panic washes over me but somehow I manage to put an aggressive tone into my voice.

"So what have you done?" I glance at the computer but I see he hasn't got past Mariette's tropical fish screen saver. I close it down.

"Nothing, I promise. I'd only just ... well ... I mean." His voice trails away.

I need to get him out of the office and into the street. "What can you possibly want from our computer and why the hell do you come on the same tour every day?"

He can see I'm edging towards the door but he doesn't try to stop me.

"It's a long story but you can help me, Kirsty. Please ..."

"Whatever it is you can tell me outside."

He seems to hesitate but then follows when I walk out to the corridor and doesn't object when I lock up.

The pavement is reassuringly crowded with tourists and local people leaving work. I put my hands on my hips. "Well? What is it?"

Mike runs his hands through his hair and looks around. "Can I buy you a coffee?" He points towards a restaurant across the road. Early evening diners are sheltering beneath an awning which flaps in the strengthening wind. It feels like a storm might be coming and I don't have a jacket with me.

I want to say, *certainly not*! But haven't I been wondering all week what his story is?

"OK, but get one thing straight: we're not going back into the office."

We take a corner table in the cafe and as my knees are still shaking a little I order a glass of wine instead of coffee. Mike asks for mineral water and takes a huge swig before looking me in the eye.

"I really am sorry I frightened you. I thought if I could just … well … I might find …"

"What?" I'm getting impatient and it's beginning to rain.

Mike draws a long breath. "Last year I came to Salzburg with my fiancée. It was all going wrong between us and I hoped a romantic trip together might help." He studies his glass for a moment. "We booked onto the Sound of Music tour thinking it might be fun but we argued that morning and she refused to come with me."

When he looks up I see blue smudges of tiredness beneath his eyes.

"I met a girl that day." His voice is gentle as he says her name. "Anna sat beside me on the coach. She was alone too so we sort of teamed up. I'd never met anyone quite like her; she was sweet and funny and …"

"So what did your fiancée think about that?" I sit back in my seat and take a sip of wine. So he's not just an intruder but a two-timer as well. I couldn't wait to tell all this to Anton.

"I didn't tell her. It wouldn't have made any difference." He meets my gaze. "She broke off our engagement a few weeks after the holiday. She'd been seeing someone at work and … well … she's married to him now."

"Oh. I'm sorry. So you and Anna …?"

He shakes his head. "I never saw her after that day. She said she wouldn't steal someone else's man."

"Didn't you try to find her?"

"We didn't exchange numbers or anything. All I know is she lives in Vienna. But she told me she came to Salzburg the same week every year and that she always took the Sound of Music tour."

"We're not the only company. She might have booked onto a different one."

Mike shakes his head. "She said this was her favourite." He gives a defeated sort of shrug. "I realise I must seem like some kind of weirdo turning up for the tour every day. But I wanted to do everything possible to find her."

"You certainly had Anton and me wondering."

He puts both hands around his glass, his fingers playing with drops of condensation running down the side. "Maybe She's not alone anymore. I don't even know her last name. I thought if I could just see your records for last year, find someone called Anna…"

"Records are confidential, you must know that." I'm feeling calmer now and if I'm honest just a tiny bit sorry for him.

He drains his glass. "I know. I'm sorry for everything. It's just … I only spent a few hours with Anna but I thought there was a real connection between us. I felt like she could be …"

"Your happy ending?"

"Does that sound stupid?"

"No. Not stupid at all."

"I know trying to find her here was a long shot but I had to give it a try."

Outside the rain has started; it slants against the windows; people are hurrying past, heads bowed against the wind.

"How long are you in Salzburg?" I ask him

"I fly home tomorrow." He stares into my eyes and I know he's silently pleading for my help.

"I'm probably going to regret this but leave me your phone number or email address, just in case." I say.

His smile is lovely and lights up his face. I wonder why Anna is a no-show this year. It would be very easy to fall for Mike Hayes even if he had nearly scared me to death half an hour ago.

I know I'll get soaked if I walk to the bus stop and there's a line of taxis across the road from the restaurant. As we walk outside Mike takes off his jacket and holds it over both our heads as we hurry over to the first cab.

"Will you ever forgive me for scaring you, Kirsty?"

His face is all concern and I want to make him feel better. "If I can sort something out about Anna I'll give you a call."

He shrugs back into his jacket, leans forward and kisses me on the cheek then strides away.

The taxi driver opens the car door for me and I give him my address as I slide into the back seat. I look back to see if Mike is still in sight but instead find myself staring straight into the face of Anton in the taxi behind. Before I can even smile at him my cab pulls away.

He doesn't answer my text and next morning our relief driver Günter is in the office.

I turn to Mariette. "Where's Anton?"

She hands me the paperwork for the day. "He phoned in sick."

I try not to look too disappointed as Günter and I walk to the coach. I really wanted to explain to Anton about Mike. What must he have thought when he saw him kiss me in the street?

To make matters worse the rain has settled over the city and it's hard to keep up the tourists' spirits as we drive to Hellbrunn to see the Sound of Music summerhouse. They grumble that they can't go inside, and stand around taking unenthusiastic photos of each other wearing emergency rain ponchos.

"I'm sorry," I say to an English matron who keeps trying the door handle, "but people kept pretending they were Liesl and jumping over the stone benches. They have to keep it locked now for health and safety reasons."

"Even Liesl hurt herself," An American woman chips in. "You take a close look at that scene in the movie and you'll see her ankle is bandaged."

Normally Anton and I have a giggle about things like this but Günter is seated in the coach with a newspaper spread over the wheel. It's going to be a very long day.

By that evening Anton still hasn't answered my texts and I begin to wonder just how ill he is. I daren't ring in case he's in bed and I don't want to speak to sulky Vanessa. It's not like we're really close friends or anything so I don't know why I'm fretting so much, but I do want to ask his advice about Mike.

Eventually he sends a text saying he'll be back at work in the morning. It's a terse message with none of his usual smiley faces and I know he must be upset about something.

As I board the coach the next morning he gives me a wintry smile. There's no chance to talk to him about Mike Hayes and when I'm not speaking to the tourists through the microphone we sit in uncomfortable silence.

When we arrive at Frohnburg and everyone is taking photographs through the gates of the house, I get back onto the coach.

"Were you really ill yesterday?"

"He shakes his head." I had to go to Vanessa's school. She's been bunking off." His voice has none of its usual warmth.

I stare through the windscreen at two women dancing along the lane, swinging their handbags and singing about having confidence. I think it best not to mention that I saw Vanessa on the bus the other day.

"Oh dear. So is she in very bad trouble?"

"She is with me." His face is grim. "I don't like the girls she's hanging round with and her teacher says her work is suffering.

Lotte drove her to school this morning and I just hope Vanessa stays there. I don't seem to be able to talk to her anymore.

After a lengthy silence I ask him how the taxi driving is going.

"It's OK, a little boring compared to this." For a second the hint of a smile darts across his face or maybe I just imagined it.

"You must have wondered what I was doing with Mike Hayes at the taxi rank."

Anton continues to look at the dancing tourists and his cool tone is back. "It's none of my business what you do with him."

I feel stung and turn to face him. "He's trying to find a girl he met last year." I struggle to keep an edge from my voice. "That's why he's been taking the tour every day, in the hope that she'll be on it too."

He shrugs without comment and I wonder where, in the space of a couple of days, my good friend Anton has gone.

Chapter Five

That evening a phone call from my mother does nothing to raise my mood.

"Why don't you forget all this nonsense and come home?" She asks. "I'm certain Jake would forgive you if you talked to him."

"You've never thought The Sound of Music was nonsense before." I sidestep the remark about Jake.

"But it's not real life is it?" she continues.

It feels pretty real to me as I stand at the window and watch the evening sun gilding the mountain tops. "I've a good job here, Mum, and I've no intention of leaving."

I hear her let out a long breath. "I don't know what silly dreams you're chasing over there, Kirsty but it's time you came back down to earth."

After the call I wonder if she's right. Maybe I am chasing something, a happy ending of my own, but isn't that what everyone wants?

My phone bleeps to tell me there's a text. It's probably mum again so I ignore it, but after I've ladled honey onto a piece of toast I take a look. The text is from Anton. *Sorry I was bad tempered today. You can tell me all about Mike Hayes in the morning.* I bite into the delicious, gooey toast and find I'm chewing and smiling at the same time.

We're back in Mondsee and this week there is no overheated nun to worry about. While the passengers have free time in the wedding

"No, we're fine, thank you. Just can't decide which of these to buy." I roll my eyes and add "You know what teenagers are like."

Five minutes later I pay for a basket of stuff I don't need and we leave. I half expect a heavy hand to come down on my shoulder as we move towards the escalator.

Vanessa's head turns from side to side as we descend. She hasn't spoken since we left the shop.

"Some friends they are," I say, "looks like they've left you to it."

"They wouldn't do that." She raises her chin but I can see tears in her eyes.

I buy her a Coke at a drinks stand near the mall entrance and in between swigs she stares at the people leaving to catch buses or strolling to their cars. Her friends don't appear. After twenty minutes I put a hand on her arm. "Come on. You can come back with me."

"You're not going to tell Anton are you?" The tears spill over now and run down her cheeks, taking most of her mascara with them.

I hand her a tissue. "I haven't decided yet. Trouble is he's worried enough about you, I don't want him to be ashamed of you as well."

She's still dabbing at her eyes when we reach my apartment.

Over mugs of coffee the whole story comes out. She's been trying to impress a gang of girls and today was a test to see how brave she was.

"I know Anton works hard," she says, "but there's never any money left for makeup and stuff. Those girls have loads."

"Only till they get caught," I say. "But you don't have to impress people to make friends. Just be yourself. Anton told me once you're really good at art. You don't want to mess up your chances of going to college just for a bunch of no-hopers like them."

She stares down at her coffee and I see, from the look of her roots, she has Anton's dark blonde hair.

"Look. I'll do a deal with you. I promise I won't tell him about today but you've got to promise you'll stop hanging round with that group of idiots."

"But they're my friends."

"Friends don't ask each other to steal, and do I have to remind you they all scarpered once the heat was on?"

"OK," she says, finally.

At the door I hand her the bag of makeup. When her face lights up she has Anton's smile too.

and out into Makartplatz. As we turn the corner Mariette is standing outside the office talking to a tall man. We let go our hands but the smile I was going to give to Anton never reaches my lips. The tall man turns and the world stands still. The tall man is Jake.

Chapter Eight

I want to speak but no words will come. Jake kisses my cheek and Mariette is all smiles. My only certainty, in these confusing minutes, is that Anton has melted away from my side. I look round for him but he must have gone into the office. Now Mariette takes my file of paperwork from me; waves goodbye and goes into the building. In the sultry evening sun Jake and I are the only two people on the pavement.

"You look ... amazing, Kirst," he says. "I love the ... err ..." He gestures to my dirndl.

I find my voice. "What are you doing here?"

"I wanted to see you ... I ..."

It's clear he's nervous but I want to tell him he shouldn't be here; that this is my new life and that a few moments ago something amazing had happened. But now the glorious kiss in Mirabelgarten seems like a dream, and I've woken into a baffling reality.

Jake suggests we go across the road for a drink It's the same café where I'd talked with Mike Hayes just a few days ago.

He orders a beer but I need to regain a clear head so I ask for mineral water. For the first time I look into Jake's eyes. I see tenderness and pain.

"You're not pleased to see me, are you?" He shifts his gaze down to the table.

"It's a shock that's all."

"I ... I should never have let you go, Kirst." He tries to reach for my hand but I pull it away. "I still think ... we could make it work. I was going to write to you or phone but then I thought, why not just jump on a plane?" He does that little shrug and half smile that I always loved.

The drinks arrive and I take a big gulp of my water.

"When did you arrive? Where are you staying?" Bombarding him with questions wins me time to gather my thoughts. Through the window I see Anton leave the office. Do I imagine his sagging shoulders? I barely hear Jake's reply … morning flight … small hotel.

Avoiding his puppy dog eyes I say, "You've turned up now saying we could still be together but I've been here for five months. I've a new life and …"

"And you were right to run away, Kirsty. I realise I was selfish, assuming you wanted the same things as me. Docklands, the parties."

"I didn't run away." I sip more water. "I just knew that sort of life wasn't for me."

"I know. That's why I wanted to talk to you. I'm selling the apartment. We can buy a house in Hampstead, close to the heath. It's a bit like being in the countryside there; wide open spaces and …"

"Hold on." I sit back in my chair. "This is going way too fast. It's … touching that you've come all this way to see me but I need time to think."

"I'm sorry. I'll go to my hotel, shower and change then we can meet up for dinner."

"No." I say this so loudly a German couple turn around and stare. "I'm tired. Jake. I'll see you tomorrow."

He looks as though he might continue trying to persuade me, but then he pulls a business card from his pocket. "This is my hotel." He scribbles *Goldener Hirsch* on the back. "Please call me in the morning."

"I'm working all day." This all seemed surreal. "I'll call you in the evening." He's about to say more so I get to my feet, hoist my bag onto my shoulder, fish out a five euro note and tuck it under my glass. Jake holds up his hands in mock surrender as I turn and walk away.

At home I pace my tiny apartment, pour myself coffee and stand at the window. How can a day begin so well and end so … confusingly? Is Jake serious about selling his apartment and does he still love me that much, I certainly don't love him … do I? And Anton, that kiss … I tingle at the memory. Was it just a mad moment? It didn't feel mad when I was in his arms, but he's with Barbara.

I can't relax so I walk out onto my tiny balcony. The sun is sinking and the city is bathed in golden light. In the street joggers and cyclists are out enjoying the warm air. It was a night similar to this when Jake and I met …

Chapter Nine

… I had taken the train to London. My friend Jasmine was celebrating the end of her university year and had hired a boat. I was on deck, cooling off after an hour of dancing. Jake and his friends were trying to gate-crash.

"This is a private party," I said, putting on my poshest voice.

"We won't be any trouble," Jake called over the heads of the security guys.

"They do look rather tasty." Jasmine said, "and rich from the look of that Porsche."

I tried very hard not to be impressed but they drove away, returning an hour later with Champagne and a huge bouquet of roses.

"Where have they found those flowers at this hour," I was trying not to laugh.

"Ahh, listen to the country girl, this is London; if you want something you can usually find it," Jas said as she waved the men onto the boat. I was flattered when Jake singled me out. "You're unspoilt," he said. "I could really fall for you, Kirsty."

To prove it he raced the Porsche up the motorway to Derbyshire to see me every weekend. He was sweet, endlessly complimenting me, singing the praises of our little village; saying how much he wanted a place in the country. It would have been unkind not to fall in love with him.

What am I thinking? Of course I loved him. But he was different when we were with his friends, talking about work all the time, bragging about the speed of his car, more like the spoiled rich boy who gate-crashed the party that first evening. He was still loving and gentle when we were alone and I even forgave him for laughing when I said how much I loved The Sound of Music. But which one was the real Jake?

My mother was overjoyed when we got engaged. Jake said we'd drive up to the Peaks every weekend once we were married and look for a nice a cottage. But when I gave up my job at the garden centre and moved into his London flat there was always some reason to keep us in the city, a breakfast meeting on Saturday morning, or a report that had to be finished before Monday.

I spent my days staring out of the window, watching planes heading out of London and wishing I was on one of them. When I went home to plan the wedding spring flowers carpeted the hills and the first lambs bleated in the valleys; all my favourite things surrounded me. I found myself not wanting to return to the flat. Poor Jake came up to see me one weekend and I sent him home with my engagement ring in his pocket. Almost immediately I saw the advert that led to my lovely job here in Salzburg.

Chapter Ten

The doorbell makes me jump and my pulse speeds up. It might be Jake but I find myself hoping its Anton.

"Vanessa."

"Sorry to turn up like this. I need your help, Kirsty."

My pulse rate slides down to normal as I put the kettle on.

"I'd really like a weekend job," she says, flopping down onto my sofa. "Do you think Anton would let me?"

"You're asking me?" I have to smile.

"He likes you. I wondered if you'd ask him for me."

The pulse racks up again. Anton likes me. But of course Anton likes me, we're friends; just friends, despite the kiss, despite the feelings that keep nudging at my heart.

Vanessa has removed the rings from her nose and lip and her makeup is subtle. As she sips her coffee an idea forms in my head.

"I might be able to help. Leave it with me," I say.

Her grin is so like her brother's it takes my breath away.

"Does ... Anton know you're here?" I can't resist asking. "No. He's at the cinema with Barbara. Lotte said I could come to see you but I mustn't be late back."

I walk her to the bus stop then make my way home, thoughts of Jake, Vanessa and Anton swirling in my head.

Next morning Anton and I sit in silence unless I speak first. I keep reminding myself that he is with Barbara and I ... well ... Jake is in the city waiting for my call but I truly don't know how I feel about him.

At Mondsee I accompany the tourists into the wedding church, trying to visualise Julie Andrews but the image in my head is Anton, by the lake with horse chestnut blossom in his hair.

Later he drops me at the office. When I've gathered up my files and handbag I turn to say goodbye and he looks into my eyes for a second. Say something, I beg silently, but he turns away.

In the office Mariette wants to know all about Jake.

"There isn't much to tell," I say, but I can see she doesn't believe me.

"Let's have a coffee," she darts out of the room.

Seconds later I hear her call, "We're out of milk. I'll pop out for some."

Hearing the door close I take a chance and sit at the computer, once again calling up last year's records for the day Mike Hayes took the tour. I feel guilty and disloyal and a very bad employee but still I note down the pickup points for passengers with the initial A, then close the file and restore Mariette's accounts to the screen. I shove the scrap of paper into my pocket as I hear her footsteps in the corridor.

"So will I be losing you as well as Anton?" She hands me my coffee.

"No. Why would you think that?"

"That handsome English guy told me yesterday tells me you two nearly got married."

How dare Jake say all that to Mariette? I take a sip of scalding coffee.

"What else did he have to say for himself?"

"That he missed you and hoped you could work things out."

"Never mind about him …" I change the subject. "There's something I'd like to ask you …"

I meet Jake in the same café and tell him I can't stay long.

"Oh. I was hoping we could have dinner."

He sounds so crestfallen I find myself wavering. He looks wonderful in a pale linen suit, his hair newly washed. I'm suddenly conscious of my tightly plaited hair and crumpled dirndl.

"Have you been sight-seeing?" I ask.

"I went up to that castle on the hill. Nice views." He waves to the waiter and orders a beer and a glass of my favourite red wine. "I've been doing a bit of work too. There's good Wi-Fi here."

"Why would you want to work when you're visiting a city as lovely as this?"

"I thought you didn't like cities, Kirsty." He grins and tilts his head to one side, a playful expression on his face.

"You can hardly compare Salzburg with London. Here everywhere you look you can see mountains. Hills and mountains are my favourite things, as you well know."

"Sorry. Let's start again." He takes my hand and this time I don't pull it away. "I'd like to buy you dinner and we can talk."

We walk to the Stadtkrug hotel and eat in the rooftop garden. Fireflies dance in the trees, the air is warm. I can't help thinking back to that first night on the Thames.

"I meant what I said," he leans towards me as we finish our dessert and order coffee. "We'll buy a house with a garden and I promise we'll look for a cottage in Derbyshire."

"You're taking too much for granted, Jake. I've moved on. I thought you had."

"Like I said yesterday, I should never have let you go. I've missed you, Kirsty." His voice is gentle. "I didn't realise how different our lives were. But opposites are supposed to attract, aren't they?" He smiles into my eyes. "I've got an idea. Hear me out …"

I bite my lip and listen. Jake wants me to go back to London for a week just to see how things go.

"I'm sure that nice boss of yours would give you the time off," he says. "We could look at some places in Hampstead. What do you say?"

I feel waves of panic swirling around me. "When? I can't just …"

"I'm leaving tomorrow; I've a meeting late afternoon that I've have to make." He pushes an envelope across the table. "I know you can't arrange it that quickly so here's some money for your ticket. Come when you can."

I stare at the envelope. "I'll think about it," I say, and he seems happy with that.

"Can I see you back to your apartment?" his eyes are asking the question I'd hoped to avoid.

"No. I'll take the bus."

We walk down to the river. I really wish he'd leave but he seems determined to stay till the bus arrives. When we see it approaching he draws me into a long kiss and some of the old magic steals down into my stomach.

"Ring me as soon as you can get away," he calls as the bus doors close. I nod and wave and watch him till the curve in the road hides him from view.

Chapter Eleven

I wake the next morning in total confusion. To avoid thoughts of either Anton or Jake I find the slip of paper bearing the names of hotels where Mike Hayes's Anna might have joined the tour last year. I look up the number of the first and punch it into my phone. The line is busy. The second is a lovely hotel in Aigen where lots of our Sound of Music fans stay. It's only a couple of stops away on the bus so on an impulse I pull on my jeans and a T-shirt and run out to the bus stop.

The receptionist is friendly; we've spoken a few times on the phone when she's made bookings for the tour. She is so welcoming that I decide to wade in and tell her the whole story. "I know I shouldn't ask but he seemed desperate to see her again and …" She listens in silence then taps Anna's details into her computer.

"Yes, this could be her," she says. "She made a booking for this year but cancelled a week before she was due to arrive. It's a shame; she has stayed here before, a nice girl."

"Oh." Disappointment floods through me. I so wanted a happy ending for Mike.

"Wait," the receptionist is still typing. "I attached a note because she rescheduled for later. Yes, she cancelled because her mother fell and broke her leg. There was no one else to care for her. She is coming in September now."

Poor Mike, so near and yet so far. Maybe he could come back later in the year. I look at my watch. I'll have to go back and get ready for work in a moment.

"I can't give you a guest's number," she says "even though I'd really like to help, and what if she has met someone else? A year is a long time."

It certainly is; this time last year I was engaged and thought my life was mapped out for me. We stare at each other for a few moments.

"He told me he didn't know where she stayed …," I say slowly, "but you're right, it is a long time. I'm sure she won't remember every tiny detail of their conversations. What if you ring her and say he's been to the hotel asking about her?"

She still looks uncomfortable with the idea.

"Or send an email? That way you wouldn't have to speak to her."

"OK," she is smiling now, we can give it try. Give me his details. I'll let you know what happens."

When I arrive at the office the coach is parked outside and my heart does a little skip when Anton smiles and climbs down from his seat. To make matters worse he takes both my hands in his.

"Kirsty, I don't know how I can thank you. This means so much to Vanessa and me. I didn't realise you and she had become friends."

The little skip slows pace when I realise what he's talking about.

"Mariette says you put in a good word for her and Vanessa is going to start working at the gift shop, here in the city, on Saturdays.

There might even be some work in the office during the school holidays too."

"She's a very bright girl," I say and wonder how long I can bear to stand here with him holding my hands, "I'm glad I was able to help."

Then Mariette arrives, apologising for her lateness and the moment is over. At least we have one happy ending, I think, as we all troop into the office.

It isn't until the afternoon, when we're driving back to Salzburg that I hear from the hotel receptionist. She tells me Anna was astonished but thrilled to get the message.

"She was quiet for so long I thought she had fainted," she tells me. "I hope it's okay, I gave her his email address and she said she'd contact him immediately."

I smile into the phone and in my eye corner I see Anton give me a curious glance.

"Mike Hayes has found his Anna," I tell him.

His smile doesn't reach his eyes. "And you are heading back to England, I hear."

My cheeks grow hot. Mariette can be such a gossip. "I haven't decided what to do yet. I might go for a week's holiday but …"

We're interrupted by a passenger who desperately needs the loo. When we stop at a Gasthof my phone beeps. Jake has sent a message telling me he loves me and attaching a photo of a pretty house in Hampstead. I stare at the picture; it's Georgian and lovely with wisteria framing the front door. Anyone would be delighted to live there. 'I've got to pull myself together,' I think. 'At least go to London and see him.'

Barbara is waiting for Anton outside the office. She is tall with a long, silky swirl of pale blonde hair hanging over one shoulder. I say goodbye to him and climb down from the coach. She nods a greeting to me and gets on board, leans over to kiss him then sits in my seat. The doors close with a hiss and they pull away from the kerb.

Chapter Twelve

Mariette is delighted to grant me a week's leave. I book my plane ticket for the following weekend and when we speak on the phone I tell Jake how beautiful the house in Hampstead looks. I get a flurry of happy messages. Vanessa is ecstatic about her job; Jake is thrilled I'm going to London and Mike Hayes emails to say he's on his way to Vienna to see Anna and he can never thank me enough. Now all I need to do is sort out my own life. I let my thoughts wander to the possibility of a future with Jake. He must love me a lot to come here begging me to go back and at least all our differences are now out in the open. Maybe it could work, I tell myself.

A few days later I sign Anton's leaving card but I can't face going out for a farewell meal with him, Mariette and Gunther. Instead, when we finish our last trip together, I give him a hug, breathing in that cologne one last time and wish him luck. We must both be thinking about that kiss because there's awkwardness between us as we say goodbye.

In the office Mariette hands me some envelopes held together with a rubber band.

"Wouldn't want you to go without your fan mail," she says.

Sometimes tourists write and say how much they've enjoyed the tour. I like receiving their letters; it reminds me that they love the film as much as I do.

On Friday evening Jake rings. "Can't wait to see you, Poppet." When did he start calling me *Poppet*? "I've booked us a meal for tomorrow night. My friends can't wait to see you again."

"Won't we be going to look at the house in Hampstead?"

"Ah. Afraid that one was snapped up but there'll be others. We'll have lots of time to look around once you're home."

My protests are brushed aside.

"Another bit of news," he sounds excited. "There's a chance of some work in New York. Isn't that fantastic?"

"New York? But what ..."

"Don't worry, Poppet. It would only delay our plans by a year or so. Think of those wide open spaces in Central Park. Bye for now."

Next morning, in the taxi to the airport, I try to drink in the view of the mountains. I've been so happy here in this beautiful city but maybe Mum is right, this isn't my real life.

In the departure lounge, I feel a weight of anxiety and confusion pressing down on me.

I gaze across the runway towards the city; the fortress on its hill. Mariette will be taking the tourists out today and Günter will be driving. I daren't let my thoughts stray to Anton.

In the pocket of my small case are the "fan mail" letters so I pull them out and tear open the first one. *Dear Kirsty*, I read, *thanks for a wonderful day seeing the sights* ... I smile, recognising faces from the enclosed photographs. One has a New York postmark and I almost laugh when I see it's from the lady who dressed as a nun that day Mike Hayes first came on the trip. She too has sent photos. There is one of her and me, but there's another one, and seeing it makes my heart do that funny, flippy thing. Anton and I are standing together at the view above St Gilgen, looking joyously happy. We're grinning into the camera in the first shot but in the second we're facing each other; our eyes are locked and we're smiling. His hand rests on my shoulder. I try to imagine it resting there now and a rush of something that feels suspiciously like ... love fills my body. Did he always look at me with that adoring expression and have I always returned it?

Then I'm on my feet and running back towards security. After a few minutes of garbled explanation I dash out of the terminal and fling open the door of a taxi. The driver asks where I want to go but I've no idea. "Head for the city," I tell him and I fumble my phone from my pocket. Vanessa answers on the second ring.

"Which bus route is Anton driving today?"

"Kirsty, I thought you'd gone to England."

"Change of plan. I need to see him. I need to see him right now."

Vanessa giggles. "He's on the number seven, heading to Aigen. But why ...?"

"I'll call you later."

As we arrive back in the city I tell the taxi driver to cross the river and take the Aignerstraße. I scan the traffic ahead and see the bus pulling away from the ice stadium.

"Follow the bus," I tell him. "I need to find someone."

Despite the weekend traffic he weaves his way until we're directly behind it.

"Is the bus driver blonde?" I ask the poor, baffled man. It must be the hysterical tone in my voice that makes him lean out of his window to peer at the bus's wing mirror.

"Looks like he is, yes."

The bus is slowing; a couple of people are waiting to get on. I chuck a twenty euro note over into the front seat. "Thank you,' I say. "Great driving."

I don't hear his reply because I'm already out, running along the pavement and heaving my case onto the bus behind a woman and her child and, as they move aside, I stare into the gorgeous, astonished face of Anton.

"Kirsty. How ... what ...?

"I couldn't go. I mean I had to see you ... I know you're with Barbara but I have to tell you how I feel. I ...

He shakes his head and even though he has the widest grin on his face he manages to say that he isn't with Barbara anymore. "We broke up a few days ago. She knew I loved someone else."

Suddenly he's on his feet and we're Maria and the Captain, in each other's arms, but instead of the summerhouse by the lake we're on a wonderful, romantic number seven bus with lots of passengers watching. As Anton's lips touch mine I know this will be my happy ending and happy endings really are my favourite things.

The End

Printed in Great Britain
by Amazon